To all children, to whom this book is affection-
ately dedicated:

The three little horses about whom this story is written are my neighbors. They play all day long in a meadow near my house, and it was through watching them, and learning to know and love them, that the idea came to me for this book.

I do hope you will like it.

Piet Worm

3 little

HORSES

by piet worm

Random House   New York

I made this book
for the children all
over the world, who
love little horses
as much as I do.

Blackie

Brownie

Whitey

Once upon a time there were three little horses. One was named Whitey because she was white all over.

One was named Blackie because she was black all over.

And one was named Brownie because she was brown all over.

Now these three little horses were the closest of friends. They grazed together in the lovely thick grass, and wherever one went, the other two went also.

One day . . . .

when the sun was shining brightly in the sky, Whitey said to her friends, "Let's do something really exciting . . . . something we've never done before!"

Then she looked at Brownie, and

Brownie looked at Blackie.

"That's a wonderful idea!" they
agreed. But what should they do?

"We'll think of something," said
Whitey.

So, to help themselves think, they
put on their thinking-caps.

Whitey's was a tall silk hat.
Brownie's had flowers on it.
Blackie's was like a clown's.
They sat and they thought and they thought . . . .
Then Whitey, who was always the

cleverest of the three, cried out

excitedly: "I know what we should
do!"

Brownie looked at Blackie and
Blackie looked at Brownie.

"Don't be so scared," cried Whitey.
"Just look over there!"

They looked,
and there,
standing in
the middle
of the grass
was an old
chair.

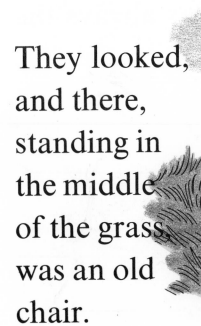

"Let's jump over the chair," cried Whitey joyfully. "We can make a game of it. And whoever knocks the chair over loses the game."

That was a wonderful idea!

So they took off their thinking-caps, as they no longer needed them, and trotted off to begin their game.

First Whitey trotted off . . . .

Then Blackie . . . .

and last of all
Brownie.

They trotted around the field, and then they took turns jumping over the chair. One . . . . . . Whitey sailed over the chair with ease. Two . . . . . Blackie sailed over, but not so easily. Three . . . . . .

What happened then?

Brownie kicked the chair and knocked it over!

"That ends the game!" cried Whitey. "Blackie and I have won, and you have lost, Brownie."

"Well," said Brownie, "it was fun while it lasted, and if I hadn't been so clumsy the game would still be on. Maybe I can do better next time.

"Shall we play it again?

"Or would you rather do something else?"

They tried to think of something else but couldn't because they were not wearing their thinking-caps.

Suddenly they heard sounds of laughter. "Ha, ha, ha!" and "Ho, ho, ho!"

Whitey looked at Brownie and

Brownie looked at Blackie. "Did you laugh?" each one asked the other.

 "Not I!" said Whitey.

 "Not I!" said Blackie. "Not I!" said Brownie. The three little horses were puzzled.

Whitey, Blackie and Brownie looked around to see where the sound had come from. Could it have been that tree? It was a rather un-usual tree, for it had a little trap door high up in its trunk. But could a tree laugh? they wondered.

"Ha! ha! ha!" There was no doubt about it now. The laughter *was* coming from the tree. What a strange thing! It frightened the three little horses, and they dashed away.

When they had gone a safe distance, they stood still, their hearts beating fast, and took another look at the tree. Meanwhile . . . . the tree was still shaking with laughter, its branches rustling as though the wind were blowing

through them. Suddenly the little
trap door opened, and . . . .
a man's face could be seen.

The man was an artist and his name was Peter.

He loved the three little horses, and wanted to make friends with them. He knew, though, that they were not used to people, so he had dressed himself in a tree suit in order not to frighten them.

Now he called to them:
"Please don't run away!"

But at this the three little horses grew even more frightened. Now the laughing tree had turned into a tree-man!

Peter tried to calm them. "See, there is nothing to be afraid of."

And he took off his tree suit.

Then, speaking softly all the while, he went over to them and began stroking them. They understood then that he was their friend, and rubbed their noses against him.

"I am so happy I found you,"
Peter told the three little horses.
"We shall have good times together,
you'll see. And I shall not let any
harm come to you."

Suddenly Peter saw the overturned
chair. He stood it right side up and
then climbed on to it.

"Oh," he cried out, "what a beauti-
ful sight!"

The three little horses wanted to
have a look too, so one by one they

got up on the chair. "Oh look!"
cried Whitey. "Look!"

"It's a real town," she said, "with
streets and houses and people."

"Oh, let's
go down
there!"
cried
Whitey.

25

Blackie looked a little doubtful.

"Do you really think it would be all right?" she asked.

"Perhaps we'd better stay here. There are people down there, you know, and they might not be kind to us. What do you think, Brownie?"

"Let's ask our friend Peter," said Brownie. "He'll give us good advice."

"That's a fine idea," the others agreed.

By this time Peter was sound
asleep in the soft grass, for he had
been drawing pictures all morning
and felt tired.

Suddenly he found himself sitting bolt upright.

The three little horses had poked him in the ribs!

"We did not mean to frighten you," said Whitey. "We only wanted to ask you a question.

"Would the people in the town below be unkind to us if we paid them a visit?"

"Of course not, my dear little horses," said Peter. Then he laughed.

"Whatever gave you that idea? But if you are afraid to go by yourselves, I shall go with you."

Suddenly Peter remembered the sign in the butcher shop that said, "We sell horse meat."

It wouldn't do at all for his three little friends to be captured! "I'll dress you up so you won't look like horses," he told them. "Wait here and I'll be right back."

Then Peter went down to the Fin-Fun Store on the main street.

There Peter bought what he wanted. He had everything placed in three large bundles and then hurried back to his little friends.

He had a wonderful surprise for the three little horses, as you shall see . . . .

They were to visit the town dressed up as princesses! Here they are in the costumes Peter bought for them:

This one is Whitey.

This is Brownie.

And here is Blackie.

Dressing the three little horses was hard work and took time. But when Peter had finished, one would have had to look closely to see that these were three little horses, for they had masks over their faces, and only their eyes could be seen.

Then Peter taught them to walk on their hind legs, for now that they were princesses they must walk on two legs instead of four. Whitey and Blackie learned quickly, but Brownie was more awkward.

"Let's not go into the town after all," Brownie said in despair.

But Peter would not hear of this.

"Come, my dear," he said patiently, "let's try once more."

And at last Brownie too was able to walk on her hind legs.

Meanwhile Peter, too, had dressed up. He was attired as a gentleman-in-waiting, with a high silk hat, a magnificent moustache, and a wonderful pair of spectacles. Now for the visit to the town.

It was noon when Peter and the
three little horses reached the town,
and as they approached the Square,
the heavy clock in the tall tower began striking the hours.

Peter noticed that a stout little man, neatly dressed in black, was walking back and forth in the center of the Square. Other men dressed just like him were standing together in a group, and behind them the streets were lined with people waving flags.

Just then the stout little man approached Peter, bowed deeply from the waist, and said, "Are these the princesses? I am the Mayor, and I have been waiting all morning to greet them."

What sort of person was this Mayor, the three little horses wondered? Would he be unfriendly?

The Mayor spoke again. "We went down to the station to meet the princesses, and now, to my surprise, I find them here!"

"Yes, yes," said Peter quickly, "princesses do not always act like ordinary people. That is why they are princesses!"

Peter had guessed correctly, as no doubt you have, that the Mayor and all the townspeople were waiting for three REAL princesses who, for some reason or other, had not arrived.

What was to be done now? In a flash Peter had the answer. His dear little horses must pretend to be the three REAL princesses!

Meanwhile, the town-councillors, in white gloves and high silk hats, stood by and bowed deeply from the waist as the Mayor introduced them.

Then the three princesses and Peter were escorted to the finest car in town. "We shall take you on a short tour," the Mayor announced.

Naturally it isn't easy for little horses to step into a car, but with Peter's help and an encouraging word whispered in their ears, Whitey, Blackie and Brownie managed to seat themselves in back while Peter and the Mayor took seats facing them.

People along the route waved their hats, caps, flags and handkerchiefs as they shouted: "Long live the Princesses! Long live the Princesses!"

Newspaper photographers
and movie cameramen
took pictures of
the big event.

After the tour, the visitors were driven to the Town Hall. There the princesses took their places on the Mayor's balcony to watch a wonderful parade. First came a group of school children carrying flags and banners. Then came the Mayor's band playing a lively march.

The three little horses were delighted. But that was only a small part of the parade, as you shall see.

After the band came a number of
gaily decorated floats.

There were also clowns, of course.

Some boys and girls came dressed as their favorite story-book characters—such as Hansel and Gretel and Little Red Riding Hood.

But who is that at the very end? It was a messenger who seemed to be in a great hurry.

When the messenger reached the great Square, he started running down the red carpet in front of the balcony where the princesses, the Mayor, and all the other important people of the town were watching the parade.

"No, no!" cried the guards. "You are not allowed to walk on that!"

"I must get this to the Mayor," shouted the messenger. But the guards barred his way. The messenger grew very angry. "You must let me pass!" he shouted all the louder. "I have an urgent telegram for the Mayor!"

Meanwhile the Mayor had stepped down from the balcony to see what all the disturbance was about.

"Must you make such a scene," he asked angrily, "and on such a special occasion?"

Without another word the messenger handed the telegram to the Mayor.

"Why, it is a Royal telegram!" exclaimed the Mayor. Quickly he opened it and read:

= QUEEN'S PALACE =

= DEAR MAYOR SO AND SO

==THE PRINCESSES HAVE A COLD - STOP

COMING TO MORROW - STOP=

THE QUEEN =

He stared at it for a moment, then turned angrily to Peter.

"Read that!" he commanded. Peter knew something terrible was about to happen.

And it did. The Mayor had the three little horses stripped of their costumes and thrown into prison along with their friend Peter.

The three
little horses
huddled
together,
crying.

The following morning the REAL princesses reached the town, and the Mayor met them at the station. They were driven to the Town Hall in the same red car that had been used the day before. When they had been seated on the great Royal Chairs, the Mayor told them the story of the three little horses. He ended by saying, "And now they are locked up in prison!" Upon hearing this the three little Princesses became very upset, for they were very fond of horses. "Your Honor, you must not do that," they told the Mayor. "Little horses cannot live shut up in prison. Besides, it was not their fault. It was their friend Peter who dressed them up, and he did it only because he wanted to help them."

"Actually, YOU are the one at fault, for you should have seen at once that they were really little horses."

"Yes," said the Mayor, "you are right."

And soon afterward the three little horses were set free.

"What darlings!" exclaimed the Princesses.

And instead of making a tour of the town, they insisted on playing with Blackie, Whitey and Brownie.

That evening, when it was time for the three Princesses to go back on the Royal Train to the Royal Palace, where they would sleep in their own Royal little beds, they did not want to leave their three new friends. So . . . . . . they took the little horses home with them!

And poor Peter was left all alone. He missed his little companions, but the Princesses had invited him to visit the Royal Palace. Some day he would see Whitey, Blackie, and Brownie again.

The End

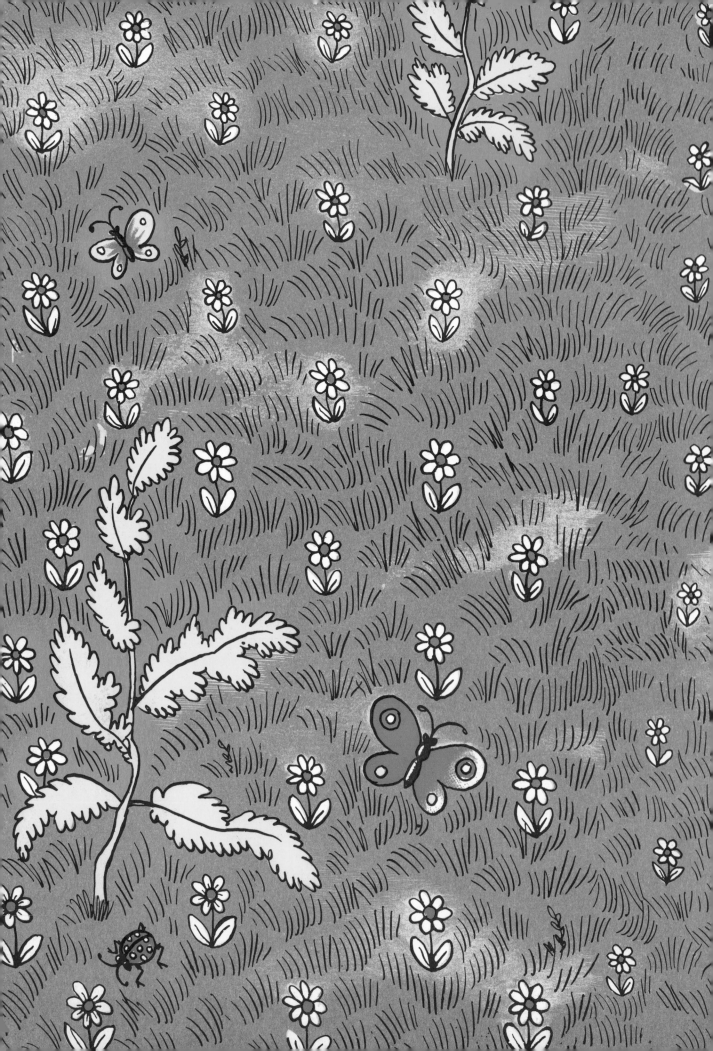